*I*n another country long ago, there was a man named
Hans who stayed up all one night

writing his play.

By morning it was done.

THE
ROYAL BUTLER & HOUSEKEEPER
ROSE'S FATHER & MOTHER

HANS HOLDING THE
BABY ROSE

THE
SNAIL

THE
PRINCESS

THE ROYAL
COOK

A ROYAL
HELPER

The Swineherd

BY HANS CHRISTIAN ANDERSEN

Narrated by Himself and Acted by His Favorite Friends and Relations

WITH PICTURES BY DEBORAH HAHN

LOTHROP, LEE & SHEPARD BOOKS • NEW YORK

TWO JOYFUL
HANDMAIDENS

THE ROYAL CAT
SAM

THE
EMPEROR

THE PRINCE HOLDING
JEFF THE ROYAL PUPPY

*O*nce upon a time there was a prince who wanted to get married.

His good name was known far and wide, so there were many
girls who would have answered his bold "Will you have me?"
with a prompt "Yes, thank you." But this prince had eyes only
for the emperor's daughter.

From his father's grave there grew a rose tree which put forth a solitary blossom once every five years. This blossom was so beautiful that it banished all sorrow and despair from those who saw it.

In the tree there lived a nightingale whose song surpassed any music ever heard before. The prince put the rose and the nightingale in a silver casket and sent them to the princess.

The princess was playing with her handmaidens when the gift arrived. She clapped her hands and hopped about. "I hope it's a pussycat!" she cried.

She opened the casket and there were the rose and the
nightingale. "Oh, how pretty! How much fun!"

"*Superbe!*" "*Charmant!*" said the handmaidens, for they all had
a smattering of French. Each one spoke it worse than the next.

The princess touched the rose. "Oh, rats!" she exclaimed. "It's
real. Why can't it be gold?" Then the nightingale began to sing,
but the rude little princess interrupted. "Good grief, the bird's
real, too. I'd rather it be a music box. Send them both away."

So the prince tried a new tactic. He rubbed dirt on his face and clothes and turned his crown backward. Then he went to the emperor and asked for a job, and that is how he became the swineherd.

In his hut next to the pigsty, he built a pot and fastened bells
to its rim. When the pot boiled, they played the old tune:

Oh, my darling Augustine,

All is lost, lost, lost.

But even more wonderful, the aromas coming from the pot told
you what was being cooked over every fire in town.

When the princess and her handmaidens heard the tune, they
were beside themselves with joy. And when the princess smelled
what was cooking in every cottage in the village, she knew she
must own the pot.

"How much do you want for it?" asked the princess.

"Ten kisses," replied the pigman.

"Goodness gracious," said the princess. "I could never allow that."
But the little princess wanted the pot very badly. "Oh, well," she
said. "All right. You ladies can stand in front so no one will see."

So the princess got her pot and the prince got his kisses.

Next the swineherd built a rattle that played all the popular
jigs and polkas when you shook it.

"How exciting!" said the silly little princess when she heard it.
"I must have it! How much is your rattle, pigman?"

"One hundred kisses or it stays with me."

For a second the princess hesitated. Then, "Stand in front!" she
cried to her handmaidens, and the kissing began.

At that very moment the emperor rose from his throne and strolled out onto his balcony. Something fishy is going on down in the field by the pigman's hut, he thought.

So the emperor galloped down to the pigsty and caught his daughter and the swineherd on their eighty-sixth kiss. He flew into a rage. "Off with you both!" he cried, and he drove the two out of his kingdom forever.

Outside the palace walls, the little princess wept.

"If only I had said yes to the good prince. Now I know what sorrow is."

The prince wiped the dirt from his face and stepped forward.

"I've come to despise you," he said. "You turned down my rose and my nightingale, but for a mere pot and rattle you kissed a swineherd. You will get what you deserve." And then he left.

Now the little princess stands there all alone in the world,
singing to herself:

Oh, my darling Augustine,
All is lost, lost, lost.

WITH ALL DUE RESPECT HANS,

WE'LL GIVE IT A NEW ENDING.

for my mother and father

Library of Congress Cataloging in Publication Data
Andersen, H. C. (Hans Christian), 1805-1875. [Svinedrengen. English] The swineherd / by Hans Christian Andersen ;
narrated by himself and acted by his favorite friends and relations ; pictures by Deborah Hahn.
p.   cm. Translation of: Svinedrengen. Summary: A prince disguises himself as a swineherd and learns the true character of the
princess he desires. After the author of this story finishes relating it, his animal audience presents an alternative ending.
ISBN 0-688-10052-X. — ISBN 0-688-10053-8 (lib. bdg.) [1. Fairy tales.] 1. Hahn, Deborah, ill. II. Title. PZ8.A542Sw 1991 [E]—dc20
90-6248 CIP AC